Rampant

Story and Illustrations by

Joshua Werner

SOURCE POINT PRESS

Published in the USA by Source Point Press.

www.SourcePointPress.com

Edited by Brittany Werner.

Copyright © 2014 Joshua Werner

All rights reserved.

ISBN-10: 0990745902
ISBN-13: 978-0-9907459-0-7

Cover art and design by Joshua Werner.
www.AsFallLeaves.com

This one's for Bre, for all the crap you put up with. ;)
I love you.

CONTENTS

	Foreword by Kasey Pierce	vii
1	The Letter	1
2	The Golden Wolf	9
3	Moreau	21
4	The Great Loss	29
5	Deep Roots	35
6	Dangerous Ground	47
7	The Next Move	63
8	The Children of the Moon	73
9	Bloodlust	87
10	The Creation	95
	Afterword: The Modern Prometheus	107
	Afterword: The Fact Inside the Fiction	113

FOREWORD

My heart races as my tongue scrapes against growing daggers. Tasting the salt of my sweat, my flesh grows to accommodate my snout. And as my dermis nearly tears at the rapid span of my own monstrosity, I lust. Blood is now heard, seen, and yearned to be tasted. Like guzzling a Satan-served Chianti, I will have the honor of drinking from freshly ripped flesh.

To surrender to the Werewolf form, is to be romanced by evil; to give into primal pleasures.

To surrender not, is a cry for death.

Charles Clerval resides in the village of Cologny, Switzerland, an area that has not seen a wolf in nearly a century. Yet, its night air carries the chill of distant howling. Charles is an upright young man of a humble upbringing in 18th Century Europe. To earn the hand of his love, he lands a job using his multilingual talents for the wealthy (and powerful) Scottish house of Wilson. True intentions, to be sure. But of course, the road to hell is paved with such. After he uncovers a dark secret, he may just find himself there.

Joshua Werner's tale of tragedy, heartbreak, and bloodlust is an outstanding homage to the Gothic era of horror. When I was asked to write this foreword, I had only 2 weeks' notice. However, this novella consumed my attention at the start. His literary descriptions created a realm that devoured my senses and left me hungry for more. What you're reading now, is an outpour of excitement less than 24 hours having read the story.

Without further ado, it is my honor and privilege to present to you Joshua Werner's *Rampant*.

-Kasey Pierce

KosmicKasey.com

1. THE LETTER

JOSHUA WERNER

On Ederachillis' shore
The grey wolf lies in wait-
Woe to the broken door,
Woe to the loosened gate,
And the groping wretch whom sleety fogs
On the trackless moor belate.

The lean and hungry wolf,
With his fangs so sharp and white,
His starveling body pinched
By the frost of a northern night,
And his pitiless eyes that scare the dark
With their green and threatening light.

He climeth the guarding dyke,
He leapeth the hurdle bars,
He steals the sheep from the pen,
And the fish from the boat-house spars,
And then digs the dead from out of the sod,
And gnaws them under the stars.

Thus every grave we dug
The hungry wolf uptore,
And every morn the sod
Was strewn with bones and gore:
Our mother-earth had denied us rest
On Ederchaillis' shore

—The Book of Highland Minstrelsy

In a time of change, in a time of sophistication and insight across Europe; when humanity began cultivating knowledge through science, when new manufacturing processes began to reshape the world... The superstitions that people clung to for centuries began to disperse faster than darkness in the morning sunlight. Black Magic slithered back into Hell... There were no more witches to burn; there was no more unholy evil to vanquish. But even in the light of day there are lingering shadows...

Charles ran to his father's bedside excitedly, as if he were a child showing off a new toy. His unkempt brown hair bounced upon his head as he dropped into the chair alongside him. "Papa, a new letter has arrived!" The man smiled weakly in reply and slowly raised himself to an upright position. He mustered an enthusiastic expression but it was immediately severed by a terrible cough. Charles felt a pang of guilt. How could he be so excited over a silly letter from his cousin, while his father was so miserably ill? He made a mental note to downplay such excitement in the future. "Ça va?" he asked, his one hand touching the old man's shoulder lightly.

"Ça va," he replied between coughs, his hand waving outward toward Charles as if to fan away his concerns.

Once the cough had subsided, Charles held the letter out toward his father. The envelope was marked from 'Henry Clerval' in the corner. He again waved his hand, but this time to send the letter away. "'Tis for you, of course," he smiled. "But do tell me the adventures of my dear nephew."

Charles opened the envelope eagerly. He always looked forward to correspondence from his cousin. They'd been more like brothers as children, neither of them having true siblings. Even after Henry and his merchant father left their tiny village of Cologny for the larger, wealthier, more populated Geneva, they'd stayed in touch through frequent letters to one another. Charles was always embarrassed of his own letters, as Henry had gone on to make such wealthy and exciting friends, while he continued to work at the orchard in this miserable little village. Henry's letter was written in flawless English, instead of their native French. He glanced quickly to his father, suddenly glad that he was the one reading the letter aloud. A considerable amount of the village spoke English as a second or third language, his father included. But few could read it and write it well. Both Henry and himself had worked hard as children, determined to speak all the languages of the region, and they'd become quite fluent in both English and German. He read the letter aloud to his father:

"To My Dearest Cousin,

I apologize that so much time has passed since last I wrote you. It has been quite busy until recent, so I embrace this opportunity to communicate a few sentiments. My dearest friend Victor has left Geneva to study at the University of Ingolstadt. I must say I am somewhat lost without him. But, of course, the Frankenstein family still treats me as one of their own. I'm often at their estate, doing my best to fill their hearts, as it is obvious they all miss Victor desperately. Especially poor Elizabeth.

I am considering perhaps going to Ingolstadt myself, and perhaps I'll follow in Victor's scholarly shoes. Just imagine the fit Father would throw. He has been pushing me towards a mercantile or commercial occupation, now more than ever. But Cousin, you understand, don't you? I just need something more humanistic. Perhaps I can find my path in Ingolstadt. But whatever would I study? As boys you and I mastered the languages so quickly... Perhaps there is a skill there? Perhaps I could learn more languages. Perhaps I could even break new ground and be the first to master all the languages of the East. I could be a bridge for so many; just imagine the commerce that would follow after better communication between regions. Perhaps even Father would be proud of that accomplishment. Oh my, listen to me, such a dreamer.

Enough about me. How does all at home? I hope that Uncle is well, and has beaten that terrible illness. You must write to me and tell me of his health. And tell me all that takes place in Cologny, and tell me more of your dear Charlotte. I want to hear every last detail!

Be well, and send my best wishes to Uncle.
Henry Clerval"

Charles turned to his father after reading the letter, awaiting the inevitable questions about Charlotte, but instead there was only a wheezing sound, followed by coughs so violent they made him bend at the waist to an upright position with each one. "Papa?" Charles' face twisted from concern to fright. As if in reply, a sound like lungs scraping along gravel barked back and blood splattered across the letter and Charles' sleeve.

2. THE GOLDEN WOLF

JOSHUA WERNER

The night was long. The fever raged and sweat soaked his father's body as he drifted in and out of sleep. Charles sat at his side, pressing a cool damp cloth to his head and comforting him when he began to mutter incoherently. The village Doctor had said there was nothing more he could do, and they'd been left to deal with illness on their own, and they seemed to be losing. The man that lay before him was not the large strong man who had raised him on his own. It was not the man that had overcome poverty and the brutal heartache of losing his wife during childbirth. This man was utterly broken. The consumption had taken all of his mass, as if his insides were eating him alive. He had all but given up on life, and perhaps he would've if not for Charles. His Papa had a kind and generous heart, and cared only for his son's well-being and happiness. He could no longer work and help earn an income for their home, trapped in that weak body in that sweat-covered bed like a man in a prison, but he always still offered a listening ear and kind, gentle advice to Charles. But his health worsened with each passing day.

The workday proved to be as long as the night, and particularly hard on Charles because he was only able to see Charlotte once, and all too briefly. Often Charlotte would come out from the mansion to visit with him while he worked. She would bring him water, and sometimes a picnic lunch, even sneaking some expensive candies from the house for them to share. She filled his thoughts, and her beautiful soft face, bright blue eyes full of excitement, and curly blonde hair made all the work quite bearable. But her visits to him seemed to be decreasing, despite her feelings for him. Her father, Alfred Moreau, owned the orchard and had never shared his daughter's fondness of the young man. His distaste for Charles was apparent, despite the best intentions he had for Charlotte, his obvious love for her, and his strong work ethic that often proved itself when he went above and beyond his duties at the orchard. It was terribly disheartening for Charles, who worked tirelessly to prove himself, and wanted nothing more than a future with Alfred's daughter.

Moreau's orchard and home were propped upon a hill in the Southwest, overlooking the small valley where the village lay. Instead of cutting across the valley to the East side to his humble cottage, Charles decided to instead walk the longer route through the forest that ran North along Lake Geneva to the West. On this route that he took on occasions where he needed extra time to think, he'd turn along the northern outskirts of the village until reaching his home in the East. On this occasion his head was swimming, and each new thought brought about a deeper feeling of despair. He thought about his father's illness and how helpless he was. He thought about Charlotte and how he had no money or successful accomplishments to deserve such a girl. He thought about Henry and all those who adored him so, and couldn't help but compare it to his own lonely life. His mind grew dark.

After walking North along the waterside a ways, he headed eastward down the wide trail that ran along the outside of the village. He stopped as

Lac de Genève
Château Wilson
Eglise Catholique
Cimetière
Verger
Château Moreau
Cologny Canton de Genève

he came upon the massive wrought iron gate that connected the fences running deep into the forest. His eyes traced along the Coat of Arms that adorned it. A knight's helmet sat upon a black shield with a golden wolf and three golden etoiles. The wolf was up on its hind legs; its face twisted into a snarling vicious look signaling it was ready to kill. He'd seen this gate many times, but something about it sent chills down his spine. Perhaps it was the wolf on the Coat of Arms, or perhaps it was the strange and mysterious Scottish clan that had lived within these uninviting boundaries for decades. It was not common to find Scottish folk inhabiting the Swiss Confederacy, and no one knew exactly why the Wilson clan had come to the small village of Cologny. But everyone knew that they brought with them a massive wealth, much greater than the Moreaus' and much of the village's modernity was due to the Wilsons' investments in the area. The Wilsons had bought nearly everything within the village limits, the land and businesses, and received a portion of the income of majority of the population each month as a result. Beyond money, it gave them power and control that few would argue with. The Wilsons were not particularly sociable, so their desires of privacy seemed to suit everyone fine. They were a prideful people, even to a fault, as even after decades of inhabiting the area they had yet to master the French language spoken by all in the region. But what made Charles' spine quiver at the thought of the Scots was not their lack of social skills or kindness; it was the rumors of their bizarre lifestyle. You see, their clan was not just a family per se, but a group of families, all bearing the Wilson name and living within one large mansion together, feeding off a large garden and herd of sheep that they kept on their expansive property. And though there seemed to be so many of them, only a few came into the village to buy supplies or settle business matters, and none came to the Church services. Some said they were all related, and that years of inbreeding had produced deformities in their children, and *that* was the real reason they were so reclusive. But stranger still was the howling sounds the villagers would hear on occasion, the distinct sound of wolves that seemed to come from their property.

It must be understood: there had not been a wolf sighting in Cologny or all of the area surrounding Geneva for nearly a century. This region had quite a history with wolves... Charles eyes fixated upon the snarling golden wolf shining off the black shield. The shield seemed to be the blackest black he'd ever seen, like an abyss, a complete lack of matter. And the golden wolf glimmered in the sunlight in a manner that it seemed to be floating in the air, feet away from the black shield instead of directly upon it like his rational mind told him it was. He recalled the tales he'd heard as a child of the wolves. And of the evil that had plagued their land...

It was they, the Swiss, who had taken the first stand against werewolves. After people had been found practicing black magic and the wolves came in hordes to kill the villagers, or so it was said, the Werewolf Trials began. It took three centuries of cleansing to reach the peace they enjoyed now. It was said that the Devil had come to the land, granting the ability to change into a wolf to all those who would kill in his name. Stories of human sacrifices, cannibalism, sex with succubi sent from Hell, and other black magic practices filled Charles mind. They said the accused people were stretched on a rack until they confessed. Then the werewolf and all family members were tied to large wagon wheels. Flesh was torn from their bodies with burning pincers, and their limbs were smashed with the blunt side of an axe head so there was no chance of them rising from the grave. They were then beheaded and burned, with all villagers required to watch. Those in wolf form were lured out of hiding at night with slaughtered animals surrounding the outer edges of the villages. A native flower that grew in the shade of their mountain meadows became their greatest advantage. These flowers were so poisonous that even picking them with bare skin could prove fatal, and it was these flowers that were stuffed inside each of the animal carcasses left out for the wolves to feed on. The flowers became known as "Wolfsbane," and were thought of fondly to this day by the locals, although they remained avoided and utterly left alone, since a plant so deadly served no purpose in a peaceful village. In fact, the nearest meadow where the blue flowers bloomed that Charles could think of was difficult to even travel to, because it lay North behind the Wilsons' land, and access was cut off by their never-ending fences.

But despite the howls echoed across the sky

from the north on the nights lit brightest by the moon, no one had actually seen wolves near the village. The stories Charles heard as a boy from his grandfather seemed almost silly, and he was unsure what parts, if any, were true. Most villagers agreed that the previous generations were too superstitious and that maybe the stories exaggerated much of it, and the parts that were true could even have been unjust persecution upon confused and mentally unstable people. The oldest villagers would gather though, on the nights they could hear the howls, and chatter about defensive plans should the werewolves return. Knowing that meadows blooming weapons in a deadly blue were at their disposal gave them a confidence that kept any from running about in hysterics. "Surely the Wilsons would open up their property to allow villagers a direct path to the Wolfsbane should their safety be threatened, right?" was the sentiment shared amongst those who worried of such things.

Charles' eyes drifted from the art adorning the gate. The soft speckled green of the land beyond came into focus as the black wrought iron faded away. And it was only then that he realized there was a large man standing on the other side of the gate. A sudden stab of fear struck him as he realized the man standing in the path leading up to the Wilsons' mansion was staring directly at him. He froze for a moment, questioning this, since the man was a bit of a distance away, and perhaps he was merely looking in his direction at something else. But as Charles squinted he became more and more certain that the man, presumably a Wilson, was staring directly at him, and standing perfectly still in the trail. How long had he been there, and if he was bothered by Charles' presence outside the gate, why hadn't he shouted to him? He decided it was time to continue on his way and abruptly turned from the gate and its golden wolf and walked home, this time at a much faster pace.

Wilson

JOSHUA WERNER

3. MOREAU

JOSHUA WERNER

Dinner proved difficult, as his father could hardly eat anything, due to increasing stomach pains and the relentless grinding cough that sounded like he'd vomit glass and rocks at any moment. He fell quickly asleep once the coughs subsided, apparently exhausted from the very experience of attempting to eat food in his condition. Charles pulled the plate away and returned to his spot at his side, wiping the sweat from his forehead and neck as his frail ribs rose up and down with each laborious breath. Then he drifted off himself, still sitting upright in the chair alongside the bed, one hand resting on his father's arm. When he awoke some time later, he was startled by his own realization that he'd fallen asleep, which was not at all his intention. He looked down to see his father was awake, and looking at him, in a rare moment of peace between pain and coughs. "Je suis désolé," he apologized, rubbing his eyes and sitting up straight.

"Non, Ce n'est pas grave," he replied with a smile, assuring his son that it was ok. "I am glad. You appear to need sleep just as much as I. But now that we are both awake, and I am not barking like *un chien*, let us speak of this girl Charlotte Moreau."

Charles recognized the look on his father's face and smiled. He knew there was no getting out of the conversation. It actually felt good as he talked about her. His Papa had always been a great listener and confidant, much like his cousin Henry. He told him of his love for her and held nothing back. He expressed his fear that Monsieur Moreau would never allow one of "the help" to marry his daughter, whom he thought of as a prize fit for a king. He told him he felt trapped by his position working for Moreau at the orchard but since there was no other work available that would gain Alfred's respect he felt he had no choice but to begin suppressing his feelings for Charlotte.

After a moment of thoughtful silence, a small cough, and the clearing of his battered throat, his father spoke. It was in a way that seemed both firm and gentle, both harsh and beautiful, an advantage that Français held over English. "You speak of respect, and wanting to be respected by Monsieur Moreau, but you are hiding part of who you are. No man should bury his feelings as if they are a shame. Speak to him truthfully and plainly. You are a man without debt who is the owner of his home, (which I am gifting to you), and you are more clever and useful than all of Cologny. You tell him this, and that your love is true, and that you wish to commit yourself to her now, so that every day after you can spend becoming greater at her side. You will not always work at his orchard, as opportunity is simply seeking you out to give you the work and wealth you deserve."

Charles blinked in surprise by this bold and profound statement. "I should tell him all this?"

"You wish to marry the girl, do you not?"

"I do, but –," Charles stammered.

"This will gain his respect. Speak to him proudly, as a man informing another of his sincere intentions." A small smile formed on Papa's face. "And think of the joy it would bring me to see your wedding and happiness before the consumption takes me."

He felt a sting in his eyes at the very thought. This was the first time his father had mentioned dying aloud, and made his illness that much more real and threatening. His emotions were so twisted together that he could no longer tell one from another, but he smiled and put a hand on his father's shoulder. "Merci, Papa. Merci beaucoup."

The next morning he rushed about the tiny cottage. He tried to find clothes that made him look respectable, but he didn't dare wear his church clothes to work at the orchard. He quickly did his best to make his hair presentable, and decided to skip breakfast altogether. If he arrived at the orchard early he knew Monsieur Moreau would be on his morning walk around his land; it would be the perfect opportunity to speak with him without the workers around and without having to go up to the house. As he approached his father's bedside to say goodbye, he saw that he appeared to be in extreme pain. "Papa!" He rushed to his side looking him over while his father clutched his sides as he coughed, his trembling lips spattered with blood. "Papa, are you ok? I can stay here today if you would prefer."

"Non," he said between coughs. "You must go, je vais bien," he assured. He waved his son off with his hand during the next terrible cough. Charles nodded, a bit apprehensively, but then turned to leave. As he walked hurriedly out the front door he heard him yell out "bonne chance!" a wish of good luck. He smiled as he walked, a new sort of calmness and confidence filled him, and it felt good.

He did everything the way his Papa had described. He showed pride in himself, spoke truthfully and plainly, and expressed his intentions to marry Charlotte and to continue searching for work that would make Monsieur Moreau proud. Much to his shock, Moreau's response bordered on rage. His teeth gritted firmly, and the veins rose up from the skin around his temples as he leaned in close to Charles' face. "Do you honestly believe that a wealthy business owner such as I would allow my daughter to marry someone who works a job that could be carried out by an ape? She needs an intelligent man with ambitions, a clear path to success. A wealthy, well-bred Genevan. Not a confused boy from Cologny living in poverty!" his voice rose to a yell. "I want to hear nothing further of your promises for the future, and as of this moment you no longer work for me." He gripped the front of Charles shirt and his eyes bore into him like blades shoved into his skull. "Stay away from my land and stay away from my daughter. Now *get out!!!*"

Charles backed away in fright. The response from Alfred Moreau was so filled with anger, he wasn't sure what would happen if he stayed a moment longer. He turned to walk away but instead found himself running across the hill that sloped down towards the village. His eyes welled with tears, to think he thought even for a moment that Moreau would accept him into his family. His head turned to look up at the mansion as he ran past and his eyes locked on Charlotte's window. She was standing there, both hands pressed flat against the window looking down at him. It was hard to tell from the distance, but he though it looked as though she'd been crying. Had she been watching the whole time? He turned away, not wanting her to see his face, not wanting her to see him in this moment where he felt so hopelessly weak.

He never stopped running a single moment, not even as he crossed the busy center of the village, not until he'd reached his father's cottage on the far East side. He needed his Papa's kind words and advice now more than ever. Not only had he failed to win the permission to take Charlotte's hand from Monsieur Moreau, but now he had no way to earn their living. His mind was racing every direction, his thoughts tossed about like a ship on the ocean during a horrible storm, preventing him from seeing the way. Preventing him from finding hope or any possible solution to his problems. He needed that beacon of light to guide him; he needed Papa's capable, rational mind that always knew what to do next. When he got to his bed he saw that he was asleep, and while part of him didn't wish to wake him, he was too filled with adrenaline and emotion; he needed to tell him what had happened. "Papa," he said, putting his hand on his arm and shaking it gently. His father was laid on his side; some small red-tinged mucus stained the casing of his pillow. He appeared to be fast asleep. "Papa." Charles shook him again. It was then that he noticed his chest was not rising and falling in that shaky laborious manner. In fact it wasn't moving at all. "Qu'est-ce qu'il y a? Papa?!" He was stricken with panic now; he rolled his father onto his back and shook both shoulders with his hands. "*Papa!*" No response. Charles shook harder. He knew inside that his father was gone, but his mind could not accept it. His father's eye lids lifted open partially, jarred apart only by the motion of the shaking, and he saw no life in those eyes. He sat on the side of the bed leaning over him, no longer trying to wake him. His voice cracked and tears ran down his face. "Je suis désolé, Papa. Je suis désolé," he said apologetically, his helplessness translating as guilt through the grief-stricken pain. "Je t'aime."

4. THE GREAT LOSS

JOSHUA WERNER

The funeral felt almost as if it wasn't real. He didn't feel like he was a part of it, but more as if he was simply watching it take place before him, like a dream playing out across a massive sheet put before his eyes. There were people, there were words, but they felt flat and meaningless, and if he could only reach out to pull it all aside like a curtain he would then see the real world, no matter how cruel and bitter it was, on the other side. His uncle and his cousin Henry had come from Geneva and stood at his side through it all. His cousin was dressed in his most expensive attire and a very fine wig, and stood clutching his three-cornered hat to his chest with his left hand and Charles' shoulder with his right. But he felt no joy in seeing his family under the circumstances. Although he wanted it to be so, he felt nothing from their attempts to offer solace. His eyes scanned the crowd to see all who had come. It was common in such a small village as this that the entire population would come out for a funeral, regardless of their feelings on the deceased. But his eyes were looking for only one person in particular. He felt a tightening in his chest as he saw her at the back of the crowd, her beautiful face now pulled into one of despair, showing a line across her brow he'd never seen before. Monsieur and Madame Moreau stood like statues on either side of her, their faces devoid of any emotion. They left halfway into the ceremony, without speaking a word to Charles. But he saw the tears on Charlotte's face as they turned to leave.

He noticed also, simply because of its rarity, that there were Wilsons present, five of them. They stood a bit farther off, away from the rest of the villagers. He recognized them, at least some. There was Lachlan Wilson, a red-haired serious-looking man with a large bushy mustache running downward to his chin. He seemed to be a family leader of sorts, their 'Chief,' Charles thought was his title. Alongside of him was his wife, a short plain-faced woman with hair the color of dirt. Charles thought her name was Margaret, but he'd only seen her a few times and wasn't entirely certain. Their son, a skinny pole of a boy around fifteen years of age, stood beside the mother. Then were another couple, a large man of six feet or so, with dark hair and a long angled scar running from beside his right eye down to his chin. The man looked intimidating, downright frightening actually, and Charles was suddenly aware that this was the man that was watching while he stood outside of the Wilson gate that day. A heavyset woman, presumably his wife, with hair as red as fire stood next to him. She looked about as kind as the scar-faced man. The Wilsons present had serious expressions, but not ones of concern, all save for the boy. He seemed to be taking in the sadness of the whole event, and the look on his face was as though he was in mourning as well.

When his Uncle left to return to Geneva, he'd noticed that he'd taken a separate carriage from Henry. Henry, it turned out, was continuing Northeast along Lake Geneva to Ingolstadt to visit his friend Victor, and perhaps even to further his own education. It wasn't jealousy that Charles felt while imagining Henry there with the Frankenstein, but rather a sharp sting of inadequacy, however unfounded the feeling may be. Upon the sight of them leaving, Charles was overwhelmed with loneliness. He immediately wished he'd tried to speak with them more, to accept the comfort they offered. But now he was left to himself, in a small village with no family, no work, and only his father's home and belongings to serve as a constant reminder of his great loss.

He had trouble sleeping the next few nights. The moon was full and as a result the room was lit much brighter than normal, with every object casting a harsh, jagged shadow. As he looked about the room, each shadow seemed to take the shape of something that weighed heavily on his mind. One shadow seemed to form the silhouette of Alfred Moreau's face, including his large ridged nose, pointed at the end. Another seemed to be the exact outline of his father's headstone. A small plant was casting the most peculiar shadow, it looked like a long snout with a wide open mouth and rows of sharp teeth. '*A wolf's head,*' he thought. At that moment he heard a sound that chilled him to his bones. It was *howling*. Faint and far off, but howling nonetheless. A childlike fear ran through him at the thought of wolves in Cologny, but he knew better. He rolled on to his stomach, blocking his view of the shadows in the room. *There are no wolves in this land, and there is no such thing as werewolves.* He convinced himself that what he heard was a stray dog, and then didn't allow his mind to dwell on it a moment further.

5. DEEP ROOTS

JOSHUA WERNER

Less than a week had passed since the full moon and the howling, when Charles was walking through the village in hopes to find work and came across a posting written in English, nailed to a post along side the church. The post was for a job working for the Wilson clan. It appeared they needed someone to work in their mansion that could read and write English, French, and German to translate and write letters of business to the Wilsons' associates. He immediately thought of Henry's plan to learn more languages to increase commerce between regions. It had seemed like another of Henry's far-fetched daydreams at the time, but the reality of its usefulness was now quite apparent. He tore the posting down, folded it, and tucked it into his waistcoat and went immediately home to write them a letter.

Once confirmed that Charles was to be in their employ, he was very grateful and excited to begin working in the Wilson home translating and writing their letters. The pay was nearly triple what he received from the Moreau Orchard, and sure to help him save the money necessary to win over Charlotte's father. He was eager, also, to learn more about their vast wealth and the sort of business they were able to conduct while remaining so reclusive. Could so much business and money really pass between entities when the primary form of communication was letters? Anything that he could learn of people in a position better than his own could surely prove useful in the future. But there was a part of him that felt nervous, and even frightened, to go into the Wilsons' mansion. So few had ever been inside, and with the rumors spoken of their strange lifestyle, what sort of things could Charles to expect to find within?

On his first day, he was met at the gate by the tall man with the scar. "Thank you," Charles said as he let him in and was latching the gate back closed. The man said nothing, but instead turned to begin walking the path to the mansion. Charles walked along side, and attempted to make some conversation with him. "My name is Charles, I don't believe we've been formally introduced."

"Aye." His voice was low and gruff.

"And what is your name, Sir?"

The man stopped walking suddenly and turned his gaze to look downward at Charles, who swallowed hard as he saw the man's stern face and the full extent of the terrible scar upon it. "My name is Malcolm. Now listen, ye should know," he leaned down towards him, eyes locked on, "I dinna want you here, Wilson business is Wilson business, and we dinna need help from the likes of ye." His face was so close he could feel his breath, which felt unusually hot. "But the decision was not mine to make, so here ye are." He turned back towards the mansion and began walking again, much to Charles' relief. "Just know, I'd feed ye to the wolves as soon as I'd spit," he said without looking, just loud enough for Charles to hear. He then turned his head and spat as he walked, as if to show to him that he indeed had no qualms about spitting. That thought resonated all the way to the door of the mansion, as he couldn't help but wonder if that was a figure of speech or quite literal. And if so, to what wolves would he be fed? He shuddered, thinking of the howls that echoed from this land that so many villagers chose to pretend they didn't hear.

Malcolm's words left his mind though, the second he stepped inside. The mansion was absolutely incredible, for lack of a more suitable word, much greater than the Moreaus'. The large entry room led to a wide staircase that went up one half flight before splitting into two separate staircases leading to the left and the right. On either side of the entry room, hallways spread to a western and eastern wing of the building. It was true then, that several families could really live in this one home. His eyes ran up and down and around the room at the upholstered furniture, the fine veneered tables, an exquisite clock, and then stopped as they looked upward at an oil painting perched upon the high wall above the center staircase. It appeared to be seven feet in height, at the least! The painting depicted a horrible looking man, with a large brow and sharp, ridged cheekbones. A small pointed crown sat atop his head, which was cloaked in long brown hair. He appeared dressed for battle, despite the crown. He wore chainmail across his chest, and a wolf skin about his shoulders like a cape. The wolf skin was quite oversized, it was clear the artist exaggerated it greatly, perhaps to make it appear that this man killed a giant beast. He held a sword in one hand, and a wide wooden shield in the other. The man looked like the 9th century Vikings he'd read about as a boy in school.

"I see ye found Prince Wolf," said a voice from across the room. He looked to see Lachlan approaching, and then glanced about, suddenly realizing Malcolm was gone. He hadn't even seen or heard him leave.

"This painting is very detailed, and very... large." He seemed to be at a loss for English words to describe its impressiveness, and suddenly felt embarrassed. "You say this man was a Prince?"

"Aye. The Danish Prince of the Royal House of Norway. Perhaps the greatest warrior of the Viking Age." Lachlan said this with an air of admiration.

He became confused as to why such an impressive painting of this Prince from so long ago would be the most prominent display in this principal room of a mansion owned by a group of Scots. "Your family, they came here from Scotland, correct?" he asked, hoping it was a polite question that would be enough to spark an explanation.

"My clan, aye. What is left of it." He said this in a way that was cold and distant, while he stared up at the painting of Prince Wolf. He turned to Charles, his eyebrow lifted and a hint of a smirk formed as he said "ye canna figure out what we're doing wi' such a painting, aye lad?"

Charles blushed, as the Scottish Chief must've seen his quizzical look and knew his thoughts. "Yes, I find it curious," he replied, "but I don't wish to pry."

"If there is something to say of a Wilson, 'tis that we're proud of our roots, to the very deepest tips in the soil." He returned his gaze to the painting, and began to point at it as he spoke. "We are of ancient line stemming directly from Prince Wolf. Norway administered Denmark, and King Harold of Norway

WOLF

saw the fire within the Danish Prince and his rowdy clan. A hungry bunch they were, rebellious and full o' piss." His Scottish accent seemed to grow thicker as he grew more excited about the story. "Harold knew a rebellion would be on his hands if he dinna act fast. So he tasked Wolf and his clan with expanding the Royal House."

"You mean invading other countries?" Charles asked, trying his best to sound neutral on such a terrible act.

"Well, their travel began as expanding trading routes, but aye, they did raid many lands and began new settlements. Eventually they reached the Shetland Isles off the coast of the Mainland." He was speaking a bit faster now and Charles didn't want to interrupt to ask questions. He assumed the 'mainland' was Scotland. "He took great care wi' Shetland, to be sure to take her greatest treasure." His eyes nearly twinkled as he said this, as if recalling from memory like he'd been present at the raid nearly a thousand years ago. "From Shetland he raided Orkney, then on to the Mainland. Unstoppable, he was. But the beauty of Scotland can capture any heart, lad." He returned his gaze to Charles, who listened with full attention. "He settled in Scotland, along wi' his treasures and brought great wealth to the people of his settlement in the North. The clan Wilson, or 'sons of the Wolf,' descend directly from Prince Wolf and his Danish tribe that settled there. Wolf gave all Wilsons wi' a grant of arms the great privilege of using the rampant wolf on their family crest."

Charles pointed towards the front door. "The

golden wolf on the gate?"

"Aye. 'Tis a symbol of great pride." He smiled slightly, then his face returned to a serious one as you could see his thoughts change course. "Enough about this, lad. Let me show ye to where ye'll be workin'." He led the way down the hall to the East. "The office is in the library in the Eastern wing. No reason for bein' in the West wing or upstairs, so ye stay out o' there," he said with strict emphasis.

"Surely, I'll only be coming here," he nodded, pointing his finger ahead at the Eastern hall.

They approached the library entrance and stopped. "Ye can find a kitchen down the hall to the left. If you get hungry, ye have full access to it." His eyes narrowed and his demeanor became more like Malcolm's than the man who had told him Viking tales not minutes before. "But I warn ye, any door ye find that leads to the yard to the North, ye must leave alone." Charles nodded, but his confusion must've shown on his face. "The North yard and South yard are separated by fencin'. If ye need some fresh air ye best head to the South yard. The North side is where we keep the barns, sheep, and gardens and such. I dinna want ye out there messin' about."

"Yes, Sir," Charles replied. He couldn't possibly imagine what harm he could do there, but he didn't dream of disobeying Lachlan. The man obviously took his land seriously, and that was fine. Charles simply wanted to work.

The Scot showed him to a desk on the left side the room. It sat next to a much larger desk made of oak and leather. There were already two stacks of letters written by Lachlan in English sitting on the desk waiting for Charles to rewrite; one stack to be written in French and the other in German. He'd expected for him to simply be present in the room and tell him what to write, but Lachlan said this was easier for him, as he would often be too busy attending to other matters to be around. He left him to the work then, and Charles began immediately.

For the first hour though he found himself quite distracted by the grandiosity of the room. His eyes kept lifting from the papers to browse about the room, which was both wider and taller than the entire cottage in which he lived. The entire wall to the right of the room was lined with books from ceiling to floor. The adjacent walls had rows of beautiful paintings, each with a small bookcase underneath. A massive bay window looked out at the South yard and he saw a few children running about there. Finally, he put down his quill and walked up to a wall of paintings. He stood before a landscape of various deep greens, studying it closely.

"Ayrshire," a voice said from behind him. Charles spun around to find a boy standing there, tall and thin. He immediately recognized him as the boy from the funeral, Lachlan's son. "I'm Michael, I didna mean to startle ye."

"Hello Michael. I was just admiring this painting here."

"'Tis of a wee glade in Ayrshire, back from where my clan came. A bonny place, I'm told." He smiled warmly and genuinely. It was reassuring to see a kind face in the house.

"Yes, 'tis very beautiful. Can I ask you a question, Michael? How many people live here?" His finger twirled in a circular motion to show he meant the mansion.

"Quite a lot of us about," he replied vaguely, still smiling.

"And they're *all* your family? Or only some?"

"Not all, exactly. Ye see, the Wilson clan is made up of a few families, all of which descend from the same land, and many of us related through marriage and the like."

"But… you *all* bear the name Wilson?"

"Aye, 'tis the way of the clan. Quite a family tree," he laughed, "but 'tis all documented." He pointed to the small bookshelf under the landscape painting. Charles eyes grew wide in the realization that that collection of books was devoted to the Wilson clan.

"Your father, he has Chieftainship. And he told me about the Prince in the painting in the entry room…"

"Aye, he and I share the blood of prince Wolf directly," he nodded, sensing where I was heading with my question. "Many in the clan do in one way or 'nother, but not all."

"Does that make you… royalty?"

The boy laughed. "Never thought of it that way. We view our clan as children of Scotland. The ol' Danish ways have been put behind us for ages," he said warmly.

"But why did you leave? Why come here?"

"*Michael,*" barked an angry voice from behind them, causing both Charles and the teenager to startle. "Ye have chores to attend to." They turned to see Malcolm come storming into the room. "Close your trap and get out o' here or I'll make sure you're not fit for much o' nothin'," he said, swinging his thumb toward the door. Michael's eyes turned to the floor and he walked hurriedly out of the library. Malcolm shortened the distance between himself and Charles in a few sweeping strides of his long legs. It was then that he noticed Malcolm's scar on his face was not the sole disfigurement upon his person. His sleeves were rolled up nearly to his elbows and an extensive number of bumps and divots were visible upon his left arm. His eyes fixated upon it for a brief moment and he realized it looked like some sort of terrible teeth marks, perhaps a bite from a dog. His eyes then rose to see that Malcolm was fully upon him, leaning in with an aggression meant to intimidate him. It was working. "If ye wish to be paid, I suggest ye get to work," he growled. "I dinna think you're here for the "*décor*"," he said, mustering his best French accent as he fell upon the final word. He then exited, and Charles felt a bit of shame mount within him for his obvious cowardice when engaging with the Wilsons. And that cowardice struck hardest when Malcolm was near.

6. DANGEROUS GROUND

Over the next three and a half weeks, his hours spent at the Wilson mansion varied day-to-day with the workload. It was all he could do to keep Charlotte out of his mind enough to get his work done. He hadn't seen nor heard from her and it was agonizing. Some days at the mansion were very short though, as there wasn't much to do, and some were quite long and filled with letters of business he found quite boring. Much had to do with the purchase and sales of land and businesses and notices of overdue rent. He saw little of Lachlan or Malcolm during that time. In fact, everyone in the mansion seemed to avoid him completely, save for Michael who enjoyed chatting with him about the clan's history. Every few days he would ask Michael to explain one of the paintings in the library, he found them all quite fascinating. The one he was most curious about was that of what appeared to be a wolf at night, but sitting upright with a body shaped like a human woman's, but covered in short fur. The wolf-woman sat upon a rock that poked up out of a stream running through a forest. A large full moon cast a bright light that glistened upon the water. Despite the wolf creature, the image appeared calm and serene. "That is the Wulver," replied Michael when Charles asked him to explain it. "'Tis an old Scottish folk tale. The Wulver was a magical creature that lived on the largest of the Shetland Islands; some say she was a spirit o' the forest." Charles recalled what Lachlan had told him about Prince Wolf raiding the Shetland Islands and taking their greatest treasure. He wondered how far back the tale went, and if it'd

Dulver

been something Wolf would've heard about. "She had the appearance of a wolf," said Michael, "but walked like a person. She'd hide in the daytime in a cave so that the people could never find her, but they say on nights where you could see clearly by the light of a full moon you could find her catching fish in a stream, sitting on her favorite rock."

"Are there any tales about the Wulver attacking people?" Charles couldn't help but compare the folk tale to the stories he'd heard about werewolves as a child.

Michael laughed. He always found Charles' lack of knowledge on such subjects amusing. "No, she was a friendly spirit, as long as she was left alone. They say she'd leave fish on the windowsills of the poor."

Another painting that fascinated him was done in a very different style, and showed two men, entirely naked except for two over-sized wolf skins cloaked about their bodies. The first time he'd asked Michael about it, the boy looked uncomfortable, and said he had to leave to do some chores and didn't have time talk. So Charles waited for a day when Michael was in a particularly talkative mood to ask again. On this day Michael seemed full of energy, and different somehow. His features had a sort of rigidity to them, as if he was losing his boyish looks quite rapidly. Small beads of sweat were on his forehead as well, despite the cool air from the changing of the seasons. He spoke quickly, and seemed to hold still no longer than a few seconds at a time, like he was excited or anxious about something. Despite this though, he was indeed in a talkative mood and Charles decided to again ask about the painting. "'Tis just more folklore," he replied.

"I enjoy hearing these tales, please do tell."

"Alright. This is an old Norse myth about a father and son named Sigmund and Sinfjotli. While hunting in the woods they came across a hut belonging to some hunters. The hunters weren't around, so they went inside. They found two large wolf skins that contained a powerful magic."

"Magic?"

"Aye, 'tis said when they put the wolf skins on they changed into wolves themselves. They spent months roaming the forest together as wolves, and they loved the feelin' it gave them. But when they got around people they couldna control themselves." His eyes grew in intensity, and Charles could swear they seemed to dilate right there on the spot. "They couldna stop themselves from killin,' they just filled up with a rage. They found the huntsmen and killed them, then onto foresters and travelers. They kept killin' until one day they got in a fight with each other. Sigmund had bit his son's throat, injurin' him. When he realized what he'd done he pulled off the wolf skins, turnin' them back into people. When Sinfjotli recovered, they agreed to never wear them again, and they burned the skins in a fire."

Charles' mind was spinning from the tale. He stared at the man on the left side of the painting. The wolf skin had a large grey stripe going down each side. He saw a skin just like this every day when he entered the mansion. It was cloaked about

Prince Wolf in the portrait in the entry room. "This man," Charles began, pointing to the one on the left.

"'Tis Sigmund," said Michael.

"The wolf skin Sigmund has looks exactly as the one on Prince Wolf in his portrait."

Michael suddenly looked nervous. He turned to look behind him; his eyes darted about the room. He took a deep breath in through his nose, as if trying to smell something. Charles was baffled, and looked about as well. Michael looked back to him and whispered quietly, "Some say Sigmund tricked his son, and burned a regular wolfskin instead. They say the magical wolfskin was passed down through the Nordic royalty, and that it was given to Prince Wolf to aid in his quest to expand their empire." Something about this shook Charles to his very core. When these myths started tying into real history it frightened him. *Why did Michael whisper? Could the magical skin be real? Could Wolf have possessed it in his travels? How did this tie into the Wulver and the Shetland Island?*

When Michael left, Charles had a difficult time returning to his work. He tried finding the right words in the right language, but instead was getting trilingual thoughts about shape-shifting creatures, Vikings, and wolves. He was a bit hungry, and thought maybe eating some food would help him focus. He decided to walk to the kitchen down the hall for the first time. He'd been too nervous to take Lachlan up on his offer to use it, but after a couple of weeks he felt now that it wouldn't appear rude to do so. There was no one in the hallway or the kitchen, despite the number of people that lived within the mansion. The kitchen was spacious and had long marble countertops; room for several people to prepare a meal at once. There was a small door on one wall, and he opened it slightly to see what was inside. It was just a narrow hallway running to another door that led outside. What he found most interesting though, were the windows. Or rather what was beyond them. From the kitchen in the East Wing he had an excellent view of a large portion of the North Yard. Much like Lachlan had said, there were barns and sheds and sheep and gardens. A man was dragging a heavy metal chain into one of the sheds and few others were about doing various yard work. But what interested him most was the maze of wrought iron fencing. The fences appeared to be nine feet tall, with rows of sharp points along the top. They ran like a grid across the yard, closing off sections from one another with gates held closed by two bulky metal bars. A fence ran tightly around the largest barn with a gate that opened to a fenced path about ten feet wide. This path led to another gate which opened to a large rectangular area with a fence-line reinforced with diagonal posts going into the ground every six feet or so of its length. A few men appeared to be checking the diagonal posts to see if they were secure. He took a step closer to the window; there was something very peculiar…

"Is it trouble you're lookin' for?" Said a woman's voice from behind him. Charles spun around to see a broad woman with bright red hair standing behind him. Her shoulders were hunched upward awkwardly and her arms angled out slightly. Charles thought she looked ready to fight him at any moment.

"No, no, of course not. I was just... just a bit... *peckish*." He smiled a shaky, nervous smile. "You are Madame Lillian, right? Malcolm's wife?"

She ignored his question and slowly walked toward him. She sniffed the air long and deep as she walked, her eyes closed momentarily. When they opened again Charles thought her pupils looked much larger than before...And it frightened him. She too, appeared to be damp with sweat despite the cool temperature. She stopped shortly before him, stared him in the face for what seemed like an eternity, then her eyes flicked toward the window. "Somethin' outside that ye fancy?"

"I was just...admiring your fence," he said nervously. "It looks quite *safe*."

"Aye. And 'tis. We protect our land well." She stepped away from Charles and positioned herself in front of the window, staring out at the North Yard. "The mountains lay beyond 'ere, 'ave to keep out the animals. Ye ever 'ear a 'owlin round these parts?"

"Yes. Sometimes I think I hear something. A wild dog maybe."

"Aye, wild indeed. Maybe dogs. Maybe *wolves*." She turned to look at him, and she was smiling, but in a way that did not appear friendly. "As ye see lad, you're safe. No wolves gettin' in 'ere." Her smile widened, and it made his stomach feel uneasy.

Charles looked again to the window, and to the large fenced area reinforced all around. Those reinforcements weren't designed to keep something out. They were designed to keep something *in*. She continued to stare in his direction, and he cursed his imagination, for it almost appeared as if her pupils were filling her irises now. He decided to carry on the conversation, anything to break this uncomfortable stare. "This land used to have a lot of wolves they say. But no one has actually seen one for a long time. How about in Scotland? Do they have many wolves there?"

"Once there were many," she said. "But they were too 'ungry. First it was just animals, then they started killin' people. Children even. The people started huntin' them down, drivin' them out of their lands. The wolves were chased out of Ayrshire, and started appearin' in Sutherland, killin' travelers along Ederachillis' shore. When the villagers started defendin' their homes, the wolves started to dig up the graves."

"The graves?" Charles was horrified.

"Aye, to feed off the bones of the dead. The 'unger Charles. It was the 'unger." She took a step closer to him. "But the wolf hunts brought people from all around. Drove the wolves North 'til they were trapped in Morayshire." She was close now, and Charles could feel the heat coming off her breath. "And now, lad, there are no more wolves in Scotland."

"Lillian, I need ye in the West Wing." It was Margaret, Lachlan's wife, standing in the doorway to the kitchen. Her voice startled Charles, but Lillian didn't flinch. "Did ye no hear what I said? The West Wing, Lillian. *Now*." Lillian sniffed the air rapidly a second, then turned toward Margaret, her shoulders hunching again and her legs spread wide apart, almost as if she were going to attack her. "I dinna want ye down this way again tonight," Margaret said, obviously not intimidated.

Lillian walked out the door, as Margaret stepped aside to let her pass. Their eyes locked on each other with a fire of an argument brewing within them.

"If ye need somethin' to eat, look in the cupboards to your right. Then ye should get back to work," said Margaret before turning and leaving him alone in the kitchen. Charles thought he'd had quite enough stories for the day, and hurriedly opened the cupboard. He immediately realized he'd opened the one on the left by mistake, and threw his head back with a sigh. He needed to regain his composure and focus. Hearing Lillian talk about the wolves and seeing the tense exchange between her and Margaret had rattled him. Before he closed the cupboard though, his attention was captured by rows of glass jars within. He felt his insides tighten, as if by reflex. Blue flowers filled the glass jars. He looked closer... it was unmistakably *Wolfsbane*. All children in Cologny are taught at an early age to recognize the poisonous plant, since merely holding it in your bare hands could be fatal. He closed the cupboard quickly. *What could they possibly be doing with all this poison?*

"And Charles," started a voice behind him again. He nearly jumped out of his skin. "How much work have ye to finish?" It was Margaret. *Had she seen him open the cupboard?*

"Quite a lot I'm afraid. These letters are quite

long and numerous, Madame. I imagine I'll still be working on them tomorrow." Charles was unsure what was happening in this house, but it suddenly felt dangerous, and he tried to keep any fear from showing in his voice.

"I need ye to work longer today then, to finish them all up proper. I want ye to stay home for the next three days. Take a rest from this place." The words sounded like a kind and thoughtful proposal, but the sound of Margaret's voice sounded stern and commanding.

"Yes, I shall work into the night if I must, Madame. I'll finish the translations and then return in four days," he repeated her instructions while nodding, hoping to make it obvious that he fully understood so that the conversation might be over. She stood there a moment, looking him over. He thought, if only for a second, that her face softened and displayed a shred of sympathy for Charles. And then she was gone.

He had no appetite left to speak of, and went straight back to his desk in the library. He tried not to think about the Wolfsbane, or the fences, or the strange behavior of the Scots, but only of the letters before him.

Hours had passed and the light of the day was fading from Cologny. He pulled the candle close, but it wasn't long before the moon was showing brightly through the bay window. He stood up a moment to look at it and saw that it was nearly full, only a sliver of darkness about the edge. There were no clouds blocking it this night, and he thought to himself how beautiful it looked when it stood alone in the sky. It appeared so large and powerful. Just then he heard men's voices moving down the hall. They grew louder as they approached. Charles rushed back to his desk in case they passed by, but the men seemed to stop walking a short way down the hall. They sounded as though they were arguing, and had stepped into the room adjacent to the library. He walked toward the wall of books like a man approaching a sleeping dragon. Each step carefully placed to make no sound.

"I canna do it any longer Lachlan! I need some open space!" a voice shouted. He recognized the low gruff voice to be Malcolm. He'd heard his barking anger before, but never directed at Lachlan. "Ye canna lock me in there again. I just canna bare it." He sounded almost as if he were pleading.

"I willna have ye with the rest. Ye know that," said Lachlan in a calm, steady voice.

"'Tis not *right*. Ye know how it *feels*. I dinna need to be with the lot o' ye, just give me my own *space!*" Malcolm's voice cracked in a desperate yell.

A crashing noise followed, like desktop items hitting the floor, and Lachlan's voice filled with an authoritative anger. "How dare ye come to me with *requests*! Ye know our laws! Ye shouldna be *alive*, and ye come to me demandin' somethin' *better?!*" His voice turned to a growl. "I took pity on ye, Malcolm. I blamed myself for makin' ye the *bastard* ye are. It weighs on my conscience, it does. But if Lillian weren't my own blood cousin, I woulda *cut off your head long ago!*" Charles clasped his hands over his mouth to stop himself from gasping. "Ye'll stay chained in the shed where ye belong, and I'll hear nothin' further of it."

He heard Malcolm storm out of the room, but without a single comment. Charles inched backwards to his desk, hardly believing what he'd just heard. He returned to his chair quietly, and could hear the faint sound of the door closing on the adjacent room and Lachlan's footsteps walking down the hall, *away* from the library. He sighed in relief. He picked up his quill, not knowing what else to do except to hurriedly finish the last of his work and get out of there. His head lifted at the sound of another crash, this time from up above somewhere on the second floor. It sounded as though someone were wrecking a room in a fit of rage.

Within moments Margaret appeared in the doorway of the library. "You're still here, Charles?"

"Yes, Madame, but nearly finished."

A loud *thunk* from upstairs caused them both to lift their heads, as if they could see through the ceiling somehow to know what it was. "I think ye should go home for the night, lad. Ye can return tomorrow to finish the rest." Her eyes narrowed and head tilted forward slightly as she looked him directly in the eyes, signaling that what came next was a command to be followed strictly. "Ye come here first thing at sunrise, finish it with haste, then be on your way. Remember, there won't be any work to do here for the next three days."

"Yes, Madame." He stood up immediately and grabbed his waistcoat. Leaving right then suited him just fine.

He left the mansion just as quickly as he could,

and counted his blessings that he didn't have to pass by any more Wilsons as he left. He continued with that same haste until he was safely home in the cottage. He tried to think it through, to make sense of everything he'd heard and witnessed throughout the day, but found that he was exhausted, and fell fast asleep, still wearing his clothes.

The night was filled with appalling images in his dreams. First he saw his father walking through the forest as if he were lost. When Charles tried to run to him he couldn't move; the branches from the trees had twisted around his arms and legs and covered his mouth so he couldn't yell out. He watched as a pack of wolves surrounded his father. By the time he could break free of the branches each wolf was running away with a blood-soaked limb in their mouth. He ran along the woods and came to a stream. He could see Charlotte sitting on a rock, though she was turned away from him. He called out to her but when she turned to face him it was no longer her at all, but the she-wolf, the Wulver. She stood up on the rock, her woman-like body bare and covered in fur, and pointed a long bony finger with a large claw at Charles. Suddenly, wolves came at him from every direction, and he was running for his very life, a never-ending horror from which he couldn't awake.

7. THE NEXT MOVE

JOSHUA WERNER

The morning walk to the Wilsons' felt long and tiring. Although he slept straight through the night, his body was telling him he hadn't slept at all, and perhaps even worse, telling him that he'd spent the night doing nothing but running from wolves in terror. Despite his exhaustion, he was determined to get his work done in the mansion as quickly as possible, and knowing he wouldn't need to return for a few days brought him great relief.

The front gate was unlocked when he arrived at the mansion. This wasn't unusual in the morning, as they expected him to arrive each day and had assigned someone to the task of unlocking it at sunrise. He'd been carefully instructed to always lock it behind him, which he had never forgotten to do. He shuddered to think of what the Wilsons might do to any unexpected visitors. As he walked up to the door of the great home he wondered if some of the things he'd seen and heard the day before had even happened at all. As if his imagination had gotten away from him, or his memory couldn't properly discern the boundaries between yesterday's events and last night's dreams. No one was in the entry room when he came in, which was common. He could hear some voices from the West Wing and one of the rooms upstairs, reminders that the numerous clan members truly were all in this one building somewhere.

As he neared the library he could hear voices coming from the kitchen further down. It sounded like a conversation between Lachlan and his son Michael. As he was entering the room he heard the concern in young Michael's voice down the hall, he sounded almost frightened. He wanted nothing more than to ignore everything and to finish the last letter's translation so he could leave. After the conversation he overheard the night before, he felt it best not to eavesdrop any further. But Michael... The boy had been so kind to him. He was the only one in the mansion that spoke to Charles simply for the pleasure of his company. He needed to hear just a bit more.

"Listen closely, lad. I canna tell you how important this is. Ye can only use this much of the flower, no more. Now we grind it up." *The flower.* Charles moved along the wall silently to get closer to the kitchen.

"Maybe it willna happen. It never happened before, maybe it willna happen tonight neither," said Michael anxiously.

"I can smell it on ye, Michael. I can see it in your eyes as well. This is the age it happened to me, and now 'twill happen to ye too. No question about it, tonight will be your first shiftin'. Canna stop it." Charles was at the edge of the kitchen doorway now, his body pressed tight against the wall. He closed his eyes and prayed silently that no one else came down the hallway.

Lachlan continued, "Once the flower is ground to little bits, we add water to the bowl, about halfway or so."

"I canna drink it, Sir."

"*Listen*," Lachlan said forcefully. "The most important part is *when* you drink it. Right as the moon appears in full, without the clouds about. You'll *feel* it. Right then, we'll all drink together, at the same time, quick as can be. *Ye canna hesitate.*"

"No, Sir, it could kill me!" Michael sounded horrified. Charles was certain then, Lachlan was going to make Michael drink *Wolfsbane!*

Lachlan grew louder, "You willna die! Not if 'tis the right amount at the right time. 'Twill help, Michael, help ye keep your wits, your *reasonin'*. And 'twill weaken ye enough so that ye dinna harm anyone." Then his voice softened and said quietly, "It's about control. Ye have to drink the Wolfsbane, lad. Just a little. 'Tis how we *survive.*"

Panic was coursing through Charles. He made his way back down the hallway as quickly and silently as he could. *He needed out of this house. He needed to think.* The entry room was still empty, but he could hear someone walking his direction from the West Wing second floor. He slipped out the front door of the mansion as quickly and quietly as he could and then ran full pace to the front gate. As he undid the latch and slipped out, he turned to see Malcolm standing in the South Yard, staring at him with a concerned and curious look. He had no intention of waiting around to see what Malcolm would have to say, as he'd certainly drag him into the house for questioning. He headed west down the trail at a sprint, determined to put as much space between himself and the Wilsons as he could.

He found himself slowed to a walk and panting once he'd made it to Lake Geneva. Lachlan's conversation with Michael was running repeatedly through his mind, but he couldn't understand what was happening. He wanted his own son to consume the most deadly poison in the land, but *why?*

Michael was sure to die, yet Lachlan seemed wholly convinced that he would live, and even that it would help him somehow. He was suddenly worried that there was a great mental illness infecting the Wilson Clan. What was going to take place tonight at sundown? Was this some sort of suicide pact, and they planned to drag the boy into it as well, unwittingly? He sat in despair for some time on the bank, trying to make sense of it all, before he was again wandering through the woods.

It wasn't long until he found himself at the edge of the forest, staring out at Moreau's Orchard. He was confused, frightened, and at a loss as to what he should do next. And somehow, on top of all of that, his heart was aching to see Charlotte, in this moment more so than ever before. He walked his way around the edge of the woods, remaining unseen by the orchard workers, until he'd worked his way along the western side of their property and had a clear view of their home. He felt as though his heart had stopped at the sight of her reading a book upon the porch.

"Charles?" She dropped the book and rose upon seeing him walk across the yard toward her. She met him halfway, her eyes welling up with tears, and threw her arms around him. "Oh, Charles, how I have missed you so! Please forgive me, I was unable to get away, but I wanted to see you, I did."

"'Tis alright, Charlotte. I understand." Her scent, her embrace, her very presence warmed him. He felt a calming wave of relief take him and every muscle seemed to relax. It was as if he had spent the morning holding his breath in, and with her he could finally exhale.

"Quickly, we must get out of sight of the house," she said, grabbing his hand and leading him away. They went to the backside of a small hill on the edge of the property where they would picnic on occasion.

"I've been working a job doing translation, and trying my best to save the pay. It – it's only the beginning of course; I hope it leads to greater things. And then maybe, maybe..." He was stammering, and his mind felt as though it was caving in.

"Charles, you're shaking!" She pulled him close. "What is it? What is wrong?"

He looked down to see that he was indeed shaking. There was so much he wanted to say to her, but everything seemed so confused now, and it was as if his own mouth was betraying him, twisting up the words before they could leave, apprehending him before he could do anything that might warrant further emotions. He tired of emotions... "The truth is... I fear something horrible might happen this evening. And... And I think I should do something to prevent it. But I had to see you. I'm frightened, Charlotte."

"What is it? Please, tell me what it is that you're afraid of. What is happening tonight?"

"I dare not say." He shook his head vigorously. "And truthfully, I'm not certain. But it may be dangerous."

"Then we will get help." She rose to her feet, reaching down to pull him up as well. "We will go to my father."

"*No*. We mustn't. I will not put you in harm, nor any of your family. I am only here to tell you... That no matter what happens..." She kneeled back to the ground beside him, her eyes looking at him with a longing for any sign of affection, despite her concern and confusion. He took in a great breath, exhaled, and summoned both courage and clarity. "I care for you, Charlotte. I am... in *love with you*." His eyes lifted to meet hers. "I aspire to better myself, to become someone your father approves of. So that we may marry, if you'd have me."

Her pale skin flushed with red about her cheeks, and she looked as though she might cry. As she opened her mouth to speak, Charles leaned forward and put a finger across her lips. "I would never wish to jeopardize a future that could be spent by your side, but I believe a friend may be in danger tonight. And I must go to his aid, despite what possible risks may lie ahead. But I will do anything and everything to be sure I come back to you. Please trust me."

She looked confused, but thoroughly swept away by his sentiment. "Alright Charles. But you have worried me."

"Worry not," he whispered, before placing his palm on her neck and gripping the back of her head with his fingers. He leaned in and kissed her with a passion that overcame his sorrows and fears, and she gave willingly. The feeling was the best he had felt in some time, and its sharp contrast to the rest of his woes made him feel it that much more. He pulled away, his heart racing. When she opened her eyes she gave him a slight smile.

He left her then, rising and walking swiftly towards the village. He'd done what he'd needed, seeing her one last time, in case something was to happen to him that night. She called after him to please wait, and when he didn't respond she shouted, "Be careful, *please!*"

Once he was across the village and in his cottage, he began to rummage, quite carelessly, through his father's beloved items. "Where is it?" he mumbled to himself, hastily moving things aside as he searched. "*There!*" he exclaimed as his eyes fell on a small wooden box. Placing the box on the bed, he undid the latch on the front, his fingers beginning to fumble with a nervous vibration. He pulled his father's flintlock pistol out of the box and held it by the muzzle. Pulling a flask out of the box next, he shook the black powder down within, followed by a lead shot. Using the ramrod stored on the underside of the barrel, he shoved it down. He then pulled out a small container and primed the flash pan with finely ground gunpowder and closed the frizzen, just as his father had taught him. Rising to his feet, he looked about his waistcoat. It was a French coat pistol, so it fit comfortably inside a large pocket. He felt somewhat stronger now that he had it on him, but he had no idea what to do next.

8. THE CHILDREN OF THE MOON

JOSHUA WERNER

As the sun began to set, Charles found himself standing in front of the golden rampant wolf on the gate at the Wilsons property. A cold wind was blowing, and the leaves danced about creating a rustling noise. He could not tell if the moon had begun to creep upwards yet, there were too many clouds in the East. The gate was locked, as he'd assumed it would be. He knew he'd have to scale the fence, so he brought a rope ladder with him that he'd made one summer when patching the cottage roof. He tied one end in a loop and tossed it up in the air with accuracy, wrapping it around one of the iron rods at the top. There was no one in sight in the yard that lay before the house, which was no surprise. He assumed whatever was taking place tonight would most likely happen in the North Yard.

He entered the mansion through the front door noiselessly, his eyes darting about to see if any clan members would be approaching. All was quiet and still, it sounded as if there was no one in the mansion at all, at least no one in any rooms close by. He made his way to the kitchen to utilize the view of the North Yard, knowing that it could also serve as means of access.

Once he was in front of the kitchen window, Charles looked out at the North Yard and could hardly believe his own eyes. Standing with their backs to him was a congregation of people in dark brown cloaks. Large hoods covered their heads and the long cloaks had the rampant wolf embroidered on the backs in a golden yellow thread. They were chanting something, slowly and rhythmically, in a foreign language. He listened closely and although he could not understand the words, he recognized it as Gaelic, a language he'd heard the Scots use on occasion.

Their bodies were facing toward an open gate on the immense reinforced fence that formed a rectangular pen. The second gate on the rectangle was closed, and four sheep stood trapped within the tunnel-like fencing running between the pen and fence lining the large barn. He noticed then that that gate functioned differently than the open one. Rather than latching closed with two metal bars, it lifted it up by a pulley system that could be operated from outside the fencing. He could see now, that this system was used to transport the sheep from the barn to the pen without ever having to enter either area.

It was growing dark now, and three of the cloaked figures lit torches in a ceremonious fashion. The chanting grew much louder now, with a timed forcefulness that created a percussive rhythm. One of the people stepped forward from the crowd then, dropping the hooded cloak to the ground, revealing her self to be a woman, fully nude. The sight of her baffled Charles, as she appeared very strange, and he squinted through the dim light trying to define her appearance. The figure was dancing now to the chanting, and as the torchlight passed over her Charles could now see that her naked body was entirely covered in paint, giving her the appearance of being covered in a short fur. A wolf's head adorned her own, and he realized that she was representing the *Wulver*, from the Shetland Island myths. Another figure stepped forward from the chanting cult and disrobed, this time a man, also fully nude but with no paint on his body. He walked forward and began dancing to the rhythm as well. He took sight of the Wulver character as if he had noticed her for the first time, and approached her with his arms out, longingly. As her head turned in his direction and saw him, she ran off a few paces in the opposite direction, her arms flying up in the air with overdramatized fear. Once she was a short distance away, she began dancing to the chant once again.

Charles felt relieved in a small way, as he realized that however unusual and disturbing this practice was, with its strange chanting and nudity, that what he was witnessing seemed to be nothing more than a ritualistic theatrical performance. Perhaps simply a mixture of entertainment and deep-rooted culture. Maybe he had misheard and misunderstood the conversations that had been happening around the house, as the Wilsons were just preparing for this bizarre play. It was dark now, but he returned to watching the naked man by torchlight, again approaching the dancing furry woman, who again trotted off in the other direction. *Who was this man supposed to represent?* He then walked toward the cloaked figures and was handed a wolf skin, the head of the wolf still attached to the skin. He wrapped it about his waist and again started to approach the dancing Wulver. As he got closer, he lifted the wolf skin up about his shoulders, and began to kneel to the ground slowly. He leaned forward onto one hand, and used the other to pull the wolf head up above his own like a hood. The wolf skin now draped over most of his body, and he began crawling towards the woman on all four limbs, doing his impersonation of a wolf. Charles realized that he must have been representing *Prince Wolf*, who indeed was in possession of the magical wolf skin from the Norse myth Michael had told him about. As the man approached the Wulver, this time as a wolf, she did not turn and run away, but instead continued to dancing to the chant. He crawled about her in a circle, lifting his nose as if he was smelling her, but still she continued to dance without running away. Once behind her the man wrapped in the wolf skin sprung upward, grabbing her and pulling her to the ground. Charles glanced quickly back and forth at the cloaked figures, waiting to see if anyone reacted, to see if this was part of the performance. The chanting continued, and no one did a thing as they began to copulate in a bestial fashion there on the ground in front of everyone. Charles' discomfort heightened as he realized that what was taking place was no longer a theatrical act, but quite literal.

The North Yard suddenly became more lit, as the light of the full moon cast down through holes in the traveling clouds. Another cloaked figure stepped forth, stood between the couple thrusting upon the ground and the chanting cult figures, and pulled down her hood. The moonlight was shining on her face as she turned to face the crowd and Charles could see clearly that this woman was Margaret, Lachlan's wife. Her head tilted back as she set her eyes on the moon emerging from the clouds, and her arms rose high above her head. "Bless the Children of the Shetland Wulver!" she shouted upward. The naked painted woman interrupted the sex and rose to her feet behind Margaret, following her example in lifting her eyes and arms toward the moon. The others continued the Gaelic chant, amplifying with the brightening moonlight. "Bless the blood line of the great Prince Wolf!" The man in the wolf skin raised then, his head tossed back and arms thrust towards the moon. "Bless us, the Protectors of the Secret!" Margaret shouted, and the chanting crowd lifted their arms to the moon as well, hands in fists pumping upward with each beat of the chant.

It was then that Charles noticed a line of people walking across the yard, behind the crowd and into the fenced pen through the open gate. They were not wearing cloaks like the rest, but instead were completely naked and carrying brown wooden bowls full of water out in front of them. Once inside the fenced area they stood side-by-side in a long straight line, holding their bowls upward just above head level with theirs arms outstretched. A couple cloaked figures closed the gate and fastened the gate shut with two heavy metal bars, locking those lined up inside. There were both men and women, and Charles recognized many of them that he'd seen about the mansion. Lillian was among those naked in the line, and a few people down he spotted Lachlan, and then Michael standing at his side. He felt his chest tighten in panic, as now feared they were going to drink from the bowls, that must've contained the ground-up Wolfsbane. Charles ran across the kitchen to the small door, went down its hallway, and opened the door that led outside. As he stood watching the ceremony in terror, the clouds parted to reveal the full, immaculate moon. The emphatic chanting intensified and Margaret screamed, *"Bless your Children of the Moon!"* Lachlan pulled his bowl towards his lips and all those in the pen did the same.

"Stop!!!" Charles burst forth, pulling his father's pistol from his waistcoat. This startled those about to drink from their bowls and he saw Michael drop his in reaction, a terrified look upon his face. The chanting stopped and all the cloaked figures and naked people turned toward him. He froze a moment, unsure of what to do next as his eyes scanned back and forth at all the people before him. He noticed then a noise coming from within the small shed off to his right, a rustle of movement and the clinking of metal. Suddenly the cloaked clan members were approaching him, the moonlight showing expressions of outrage on their faces. "Stay back!" he shouted, waving his pistol about in front of him at each of his aggressors. "If anyone comes any closer I'll shoot them right in the head!" They responded appropriately, each taking a few steps back slowly. Charles began walking around them towards the gate on the fence, careful to face the angry crowd at all times.

Once he'd walked backwards to the gate, he heard Lachlan growl at him in anger, "Wha' the hell are ye doin' *ye damn fool?*"

Charles replied loudly for all to hear, in the bravest voice he could muster, "I can't let you poison Michael! I'm taking him out of here *right now*, and the first person who tries to stop me will have a *lead ball in their skull!*" He waved the flintlock from the slowly approaching crowd to the people in the pen and then back to the crowd. He tried not to show his panic to the Wilsons, although he knew full well he'd only be able to get one shot off. There was no way this mob would give him enough time to reload. It seemed hopeless, but he had to try.

"May the devil cut the head off ye and make a day's work of your neck!" spat Lachlan as Charles lifted the bottom of the two metal bars on the gate, eyes still on the crowd closing in.

"Michael, get over here! I'm getting you out of this place," said Charles, his eyes darting to the naked boy whose expression of fear was now turning to one of anguish and pain. "Michael? Are you alright?" The boy dropped to his knees, his head tilted back and his eyes opened wide with terror. He began to claw at himself, digging his fingertips into his face, all the while screaming out in pain. Charles looked back to the cloaked crowd that had planned to attack him the first opportunity they had, but now they inched backwards away from the gate. His eyes shot back to Michael, who had now thrown his face to the ground and was frantically slapping at clawing at his own back, as if his very skin was now a deadly enemy. "What- what's w-wrong?" Charles voice was shaking now; he was so far under in this mess he felt he'd never resurface for air, and a dreadful angst was overwhelming him. "Did they poison you?" he asked weakly. Michael's only reply was an unintelligible howl. Charles waved the gun at Lachlan and the other naked Scots in the pen and began to lift the second bar holding the gate closed.

The others in the pen began to writhe in anguish abruptly, and Charles stopped unlatching the gate, now completely unsure of what to do. A groan followed by a painful yell came from the small shed off to the side, and then the sound of metal clanking rapidly. The clansmen in the pen were all on the ground now, rolling, squirming, twitching, and pulling at their skin. "Oh God, tell me what to do! What can I do to help?!" he shouted frantically. He looked to Margaret, but she was backing away, her eyes wide and staring at the undone latch on the bottom half of the gate. It was then that he saw Michael's flesh tear open along his spine, and dark fur poked out from underneath. He grabbed his nose, two fingers up into his nostrils, and yanked upward, tearing his lips and surrounding skin clean off, until a muzzle grew forth underneath and his entire face shredded away. Charles was frozen in horror as Lachlan and all of the clansmen changed before him, as if their very bodies were simply costumes that could be torn off so that a beast underneath could emerge.

The beast rising from within Michael lurched forward and rammed into the gate, its new head covered in blood and dripping bits of flesh rose upward to meet eyes with Charles. It was the head of a *wolf*. Michael's hand shot outward through the opening in the lower half the gate and grabbed Charles' leg, but only a moment later his fingers flopped loosely across the back of his hand and a dark fur-covered paw emerged, ripping its claws into Charles skin and tearing him from knee to ankle. He fell backward screaming in pain, as the tall dark wolf shook loose the remnants of Michael's human flesh like a dog would shake off water. He looked up to see all the Scots in the pen were now wolves, nearly twice the size of normal ones, covered in blood and bits of the skin that had laid over them only a minute before.

Charles squirmed, pushing himself backward with his feet and one arm, the other now aiming the gun at the wolves charging the wrought iron gate. Their bodies rammed against it, one after the other in a frenzy. Some wolves were climbing over one another to claw at the gate, all of them trying to get at him with a ferocious desire to kill. He pointed the pistol forward, unsure of which wolf to shoot and terrified he'd waste his only shot, as he heard the clanging of metal and wood in a violent shaking. He glanced to the small shed, which was nearly rocking side to side with a great powerful force. He now aimed his pistol in the shed's direction, certain that something would burst forth from there any second to devour him. A loud groan of buckling iron came forth as the wolves pounded into the gate, and the bottom half now bent far enough open that Michael's wolf emerged. He swung his gun toward the wolf and pulled the trigger, a resounding blast erupting. The wolf's left shoulder jerked backward but its body was already bounding towards him and it hardly slowed the beast down. It pinned Charles to the ground and sunk its teeth into his shoulder

Loup-Garou

and began ripping back and forth in quick violent jerks. He howled in pain and flailed about, trying to get loose from the wolf's teeth, dropping his flintlock in the process. Its jaws were too strong and its weight too heavy, Charles was pinned down and couldn't move enough to get free.

A thundering roar came from his right and the door of the shed erupted forward in a spray of splintered wood chunks. A creature sprang forth, tackling Michael's wolf with the strength of a horse running at full speed. Charles thought at first that it was a man, but then saw it was a *monstrosity*. It appeared to have a man's body and wore pants, but no other clothing, and his exposed skin was covered in a long fur-like hair. Charles was frozen in fear, and watched as the creature pinned the massive wolf on its side to the ground, using its knee and clawed hands. The face was disfigured; not a man's face but not a wolf's either. It was somewhere in-between, with a thick heavy brow and mouth and nose extended into a short muzzle. Parts of the face were a tan flesh and other parts covered in patches of fur. And then he saw it, the scar running down the side of the face. *Malcolm's scar*.

"Get ahold of that man, we have to *kill him!*" a voice shouted unapologetically. It was Margaret, and she was pointing directly at Charles. "He'll be a bastard for sure. Finish 'im off!" He scrambled to his feet as the cloaked Scots approached, but more wolves were escaping the pen now through the bent gate. Two of the wolves went straight for the wolf-man, tearing at his limbs. The others started running toward the cloaked Wilsons, who stopped coming after Charles and instead began running across the yard in terror. Amidst the chaos, growls, and horrific screams, he saw this is as his only opportunity to escape. He sprinted to the small door that led to the kitchen entrance, and could hardly believe he'd made it once inside. Once in the kitchen he glanced back out the window only for a brief moment, to see the wolf-man Malcolm having his throat torn out and clan members being chased down by the abominations given creation by a madman with too much power and an ancient spirit of the forest. He started running then, and didn't dare look behind him once more.

9. BLOODLUST

JOSHUA WERNER

Through the mansion, across the South Yard, out the gate, down the path, into the woods. His lungs burned as the cool night air shot in and out. As the adrenaline began to wear off, the pain set in and Charles was suddenly much more aware of his shredded trousers wet with blood and the throbbing sensation in his shoulder where mighty teeth had torn through his waistcoat and linen shirt and deep into his skin. He heard the howls then, the long howls directed at the luminous moon, the wolves. He pressed on.

When Charles collapsed on the ground he was unsure of where his body had even taken him. His leg ached from the deep gouges from Michael's claws, but it didn't compare to the unprecedented burning he now felt raging through the area surrounding the bite on his shoulder. He knew he couldn't get up off the ground, he felt as though he may not even remain conscious much longer, but he reached to the hole torn in his waistcoat and tugged downward, ripping it further. He slid his hand inside and felt his skin near the bloodied teeth marks. It was hot to the touch, hotter than his father's fevers had ever been. He felt his mind getting fuzzy, and lifted his head to look upward, doing his best to make his eyes focus. It was the Moreau mansion up ahead; he had run all the way to the orchard. He thought he saw something then, a person appearing on the porch of the house, were they calling to him? The house seemed to slip backwards in space, it suddenly felt so far away, and then it was only darkness.

When he opened his eyes he was on his back,

and he saw a small cloud passing across the radiant totality of the moon. Blonde curls interrupted it then, inching across his view until the brilliant light was replaced with the face of the woman he loved. She looked horrified.

"Oh Charles, what has happened? *What did this to you?*" Charlotte cried, her hands upon the sides of his face.

He opened his mouth to speak, but his throat felt terribly coarse. He tried to lift himself upward, and it seemed as though each of the muscles in his body were pulling at once, stretching themselves agonizingly thin. He looked back to the moon, and it was full again, no clouds to block its light. Charlotte had torn off a piece of her dress now and was pressing it to his shoulder. His face felt as if it were swollen, his skin hot and tight. He ran his fingers along his cheeks and his nose, inspecting each feature with his fingertips as the sensation of swelling increased. An excruciating pain caused him to suddenly spasm, and jerk away from Charlotte. His very bones felt as if they were shifting, grinding across one another.

"What is it? Charles! What's wrong?" Charlotte was sobbing now as she saw his body writhing in torment. "I'm going to the house to get help!" she said, jumping to her feet.

"Wait..." Charles whispered. He felt his teeth shifting in his mouth now, he could barely speak through the strange feeling of his jaws grinding along one another. He lifted a hand out to her but she was already turned toward the house and had begun running across the yard. "Char-," he tried to make his mouth work properly. "Were – *Werewolves!*" he grunted. He pushed himself up to his feet, determined to warn her properly, but noticed his own arms were changing before his eyes. Thick long hair was sprouting down his arms and across his hands, which looked bony and knotted like an old tree. His fingernails had turned into black claws protruding and extending from his fingers. An image flashed in his mind of Malcolm, and his hairy disfigured appearance. Malcolm the *bastard*. Malcolm the *wolf-man*. He began to panic, and as he looked at Charlotte running up to the house for help, she suddenly looked different to him. The panic faded as he watched her legs moving swiftly, one after the other. Something about her muscles in motion excited him. He felt a surge of energy run through him and began to run, to chase after her, with incredible new strength he'd never felt before. As the distance shortened between them rapidly, he heard something new, a thumping sound repeating and pounding into his ears, Charlotte's heartbeat. He felt roused, he felt lustful, he felt *hungry*. He watched as the veins in her neck moved as she ran and was overcome with the compulsion to open them up, to feel the heat of her insides, to feel the pressure of her blood shoved forth by her strong beating heart. He stretched his mouth open to feel his new jaws as he ran on his new limber feet. He felt the moon's light wash over him, permeating him with vigor.

Charlotte realized he was running behind her now, and turned back to look. Her screams served no purpose, as Charles leapt upon her and tore at

homme-Loup

her throat with his teeth, other than to alert those inside the house. He felt nothing but the hunger as he pulled her meat from her bones. His appetite was not just a literal one for flesh and blood, but also for the thrill of the hunt. It was all-consuming like a blind rage, like a seething hatred for every living thing, even those whom he loved most. Perhaps the most disgusting part of this rage was how good it felt, to be both destructive and enraged and utterly pleasured simultaneously.

When the sound of screaming and shouting met his ears from those running out of the house, an animal-like instinct overcame him to bound off through the night. As he ran through the woods he heard their words but could hardly seem to decipher their meaning.

"Dear Lord, *Charlotte!*"

"Did you see what it was?"

"Oh God!"

"I saw its shape in the moonlight, 'twas not human I tell you!"

"Charlotte, *wake up!*"

"Some kind of beast, it went running into the forest!"

"Charlotte!"

"Charlotte!!!"

10. THE CREATION

JOSHUA WERNER

As the Creation walked through the woods along the Lake Geneva shore he was mindful of where he was on the map that he'd taken. Holding it upward into a beam of moonlight falling between the trees, he ran one of his fingers along the word 'Geneva.' He moved his lips silently, making the shape necessary to pronounce each syllable. The Creation wondered, then, how much of his rapid learning was because of the stray memories that kept forcing their way into his mind, and not a result of his constant attempts to better his speech and reading through mimicry. Some of the other words on the map he couldn't read at all, but *Geneva* screamed off the page to him.

As the eight-foot-tall monster of a man lumbered through the forest he folded the map back up and put it inside his pocket. The light of the moon cast down upon his hands, drawing attention to the grotesque scar wrapping around his wrist where it'd been sewn to the forearm. His pale skin was of a yellow hue, and seemed thin and transparent, barely covering the work of muscles and arteries so meticulously put together underneath. He was a living corpse. A single thought passed through the Creation's mind as he looked upon his own hands and arms, *'Why?'*

As he continued onward his mind was anchored with dejection. He thought of his creator, his 'father' of sorts, and the infinite disgust and dismay he projected upon seeing what he had made. *Why?* His emotions were uncontrollable, and with each thought he felt as though he were reliving the experience. With a shaking hand he reached into the interior pocket of his long jacket and felt the folded pages of his father's journal, and wept. He thought about the DeLacey family, and all he'd learned by observing them. And of the deep empathy he felt, the shared sorrow. All to be shunned and driven away when he tried to befriend them. *Why?* He rocked forward with the deep sobs that spurt forth. He wrapped his arms about himself, clutching both arms with the opposite hand, wanting to feel warmth, wanting to feel comfort, longing for a friendly touch. As his fingers came close to the wound in his shoulder he felt a sting of pain, and he thought of the girl he had seen drowning, the girl he had so selflessly saved, just to be shot with a pistol instead of met with thanks. He remembered the horrible, unimaginable pain. He remembered his confusion and fright, with no one to explain to him what was happening. No one to tell him *why*. And he grew angry. His weeping stopped, and the rejection he felt turned to hatred. Hatred for all who had shunned him, hatred for a man who would create him and then turn him away terror-stricken and disconcerted, with no knowledge or skills to survive. He pounded his fists against a tree and let out a roar of resentment.

He lifted his head from the side of the tree as he heard a noise nearby in the forest. His watery glowing eyes skimmed the surrounding trees, and then he heard it again, the slight rustle of leaves and the snap of a branch. He spun around to see a man-like creature, with a blood-covered face like that of a wolf, all covered in hair, come bounding toward him. The creature was feral, teeth gnashing and arms outstretched before it swiping its claws through the air. The Creation dashed forward, meeting its speed and strength head-on. As the animal clawed at him it scraped upon the wound on his shoulder, sending a jolt of pain through him. He grabbed it up by its torso, throwing it down to the ground with the might of his own body weight upon it. His hands formed fists and began to pummel the wolf-man's face. Upon the second impact the clouds began to pass over the moon, obstructing the light. The Creation thought he saw the creature's face begin to change shape then, but he pounded his fists down on it again in a rage. The wolf-man was no longer moving, but again he threw his fists down upon it. When he lifted his hands again he saw that it looked different, that he was hitting an ordinary man. He hurled himself backward off the unconscious man, bewildered at the sight. Had he imagined the sharp teeth, the muzzle, the hair, the claws? He looked to his shoulder where he saw fresh rips in his jacket and felt them to be certain they were real.

After a moment the man on the ground began to stir. The man-made monster kneeled down at his side, concerned and feeling regret for the beating he had just delivered. As the weakened man opened his eyes and looked up at the colossal looming figure, he strained to focus his vision. When his eyes had adjusted they traced along the scars running between the areas where pieces of corpses had been stitched together. He saw the dark, decayed lips contrasting the pale yellowish skin, and his breathing sped up in alarm. The Creation held his hands out, fingertips raised upward, and rotated them side-to-side in an instinctual signal for the man not to be frightened. The man pushed himself away backwards on his hands until his back reached a tree, where he pinned himself as he took in the sight of this massive abhorrent man. The Creation moved from a kneeling position to sitting on his bottom, his legs crossed in front of him. He sat in silence, allowing the frightened man to acclimate to his appearance. The man calmed down and his panting breath slowed, as he realized no danger was going to befall.

The man rubbed his chin with the back of his hand, and upon realizing it was wet, looked curiously at it. The man-made monster watched the man's eyes grow wide with the realization that it was blood, and then saw him break into a far-off stare, as if reliving something in his mind. And if the man's expressions were to be of any indication, it was something truly appalling. The man's face crinkled up as his eyes glossed with tears and his breath began to jerk in and out shakily. He began slapping at his mouth violently, trying to wipe the blood off of him as if he was terrified of it. "Oh God!" the man groaned as he fell to his side in the leaves. *"God!"* he wailed. "What have I *done?*" the last of his words shook in and out with his racking sobs. Moans of grief turned to a hacking sound, and the man began to vomit blood and small wet chunks of body tissue. As he wept in a puddle of his bloody vomit, the Creation watched him, an empathetic compassion forming within him. Here was a man in pain, but he did not know how to help.

After a while the man grew silent and still, and had once again propped his back against a tree. He looked as though his mind was betraying his sensibilities, as though it was shutting off his ability to feel any further emotions in an attempt to protect him. The Creation stood and walked over to him, bent down, and held out a flask. The man looked to the flask and then up to the monstrous face, and the monster spoke, "Water."

He took the flask, unscrewed the cap, and took a long drink. When he handed it back he said, "Thank you." His voice was gruff, and he cleared his throat with a strong cough, then repeated, "*Thank you*. My name is Charles." After a second of silence he asked, "What is yours, Sir?"

The Creation's voice was coarse, like one made low and rugged from an illness. "I... have no name."

"You have no name? But how is that possible? What do others call you?"

"My... father... *rejected* me, before giving me a name," the monster said slowly.

A thoughtful look crossed over his face, and it was clear that he didn't understand, but didn't press further on the subject. "And you are traveling alone?" Charles asked softly.

"Yes. Others... They are afraid of me." He moved his hand in a circular motion in front of his face with his fingers spread out, indicating the fear was due to his looks. "I travel to Geneva. To learn more... about where I come from. About *who I am*." His gaze cast downwards to the ground. "They call me... a devil... a monster. But I mean you no harm..."

Charles glanced over the man again, and then his eyes went lifeless, as he appeared to pull within himself. "You are not the monster here," he said quietly. He looked up to meet the Creation's eyes, leaned forward and said, "I have done horrible, *horrible* things tonight." His face wrinkled into a hard frown. "Things I could not control. Things that sicken me, that disgust my very soul." Again, he quietly added, "I am the monster here." His voice reached high in pitch as he suppressed another sob, "I have killed the woman I love. *I killed her*."

Charles' brow wrinkled with sudden concern. He rose to his feet and began pushing his fingers lightly into the flesh of his face. He looked upward to the moon to see that the clouds were parting way; the moonlight was growing in strength again. He gasped at the sight, and the monster looked upward as well, confused. In the distance they could hear shouting now, and both creatures of despair turned their heads toward the sound. They heard branches cracking and could see the flickering of torchlights. As the sounds grew closer they could tell it was several people. A voice yelled out "I think it ran this way!"

"You have to get out of here, *now!*" Charles said, his eyes moving from the monster to the moon and back. The Creation did not move, but simply stared at Charles in wonder. "Go! I'm going to – to change. Into a beast, and I will kill you, surely!" He ran to the eight-foot-tall man and shoved him in the chest, *"Get out of here!"* His voice was beginning to change, it sounded muffled as if his mouth was unable to make all the correct shapes.

The Creation did not move, its body not even flinching from the push. "You look like a man... who needs *help*," he said.

Charles stopped a moment, taking in the massive might of him. "You *can* help me." His face wore an expression of extreme desperation. "You can *kill me*." The monster took a step backward, it's head shaking side-to-side in small motions. "You must. You have the strength!" Charles grabbed the monster's wrists and lifted the giant hands to his throat. He winced in pain as his body began the changes. His teeth shifted and began to protrude in an under bite, and growled forth "Stop me from hurting anyone else. Stop me from killing again!"

The Creation looked off into the woods as the voices came closer, then back to his hands around the throat of this pathetic man writhing in pain. "No..." he said. "Don't make do this." Fur began to sprout from Charles' cheeks and his hands began changing shape. He could hardly believe his eyes.

"Do it," Charles growled, gripping the scarred wrists tighter. *"Please!"*

The monster looked to the flickering torches and could see the faint outline of the people now.

"Up ahead! I think I see something over there!"

"Is it the beast that killed Charlotte?"

The wolf-man's grip on his wrists grew tighter, and his fingers turned to sharp claws that were digging into him now. He felt the heat of his throat upon the palms of his hand, and then the sharp pain of the claws cutting into him. "I am not a *murderer*," he grunted.

"I see it! What the hell is that thing?!" a voice yelled out from enclosing mob.

The pain grew and the wolf-man snarled and began to kick. The moon shone bright and the angry mob approached. Emotions filled him, and he felt no control.

And then the monster simply closed his fingers inward. Charles' throat was crushed, and a gagging noise came out his muzzle. He'd made both hands into fists, and without opening them again Charles fell backward, a spray of blood erupting from the hole in his neck. The Creation's hands were shaking and he straightened his fingers out once more, the meat of the wolf-man's throat falling to the ground. He looked down to Charles' dead body and saw that the horrific beast-features were fading fast; his corpse would be that of the man he was, and not the creature he had became.

"Oh Lord! It's a *monster!* And he's killed *another* one!" shouted a villager, and the Creation knew it was once again time to run.

And so he ran, as fast as his towering legs could move. And a darkness shrouded his mind, as he realized killing was not as hard as he'd expected. He was alone again, abandoned in his father's exile. But his purpose was renewed, he wanted *revenge*. So he ran hard, toward Geneva. Toward the home of Victor Frankenstein.

The End.

AFTERWORD: THE MODERN PROMETHEUS

Why the Frankenstein connection?

Rampant, or at least the last chapter of it, is loosely based on a comic book script I wrote years ago called *"The Monster Meets the Wolf-man."* It was intended to be a 1-shot comic where I could dig in and express my love for some of my favorite horror icons, but I didn't continue the comic book after penciling and inking the first three pages as I didn't feel like the script was properly developed and the story focused primarily on Frankenstein's monster, or as I affectionately refer to him in *Rampant*, 'the *Creation*.' The comic book was intended to basically be the last chapter of this story, about a suicidal wolf-man running in to the monster in the forest, and the comic gave them more time together to form a bond and friendship, but ultimately ended in the same fashion as Rampant. With that comic book script I knew I wanted to tell a dark, serious, and emotional story but I eventually abandoned it for other projects, as I felt it simply wasn't my best work.

With *Rampant*, I approached this quite differently initially. I wanted to write a werewolf short story (which soon grew into a novella), but I took it upon myself to attempt to create a brand new origin entirely, one explaining where werewolves came from. As I developed my ideas and did my research, I suddenly realized this project was becoming a bit ambitious, and it was likely to become quite a long 'short story.' Having accepted that I planned to devote endless hours to bringing a narrative to my ideas, I decided to make the challenge greater by writing a story that was both in a different time period and also a different country. And to both thrill myself and create additional stress for myself, I decided then to add another layer of complexity to this story by attempting a seamless direct tie-in to Mary Shelley's *Frankenstein*.

To properly prepare the reader for the tie-in and to also help the reader feel comfortable with the setting and time period, I felt it important to establish Charles' direct connection to Mary Shelley's character Henry Clerval in the first chapter. From there I strived to create a story that did not require extensive knowledge of her novel to make the tie-in effective, but to also create a story that could be enjoyed that much more by readers who are quite familiar with her novel. I felt a connection between the sorrow and loss presented in *Frankenstein*, and the tragic tale I was spinning of my own.

The story takes place somewhere in the 1790s, as Mary Shelley's novel was set. Readers familiar with that novel will find that Charles' tale takes place at a very specific time in her book, and acts as a transitional moment for the monster. In *Frankenstein*, Henry arrives in Ingolstadt shortly after Victor brought the monster to life and then immediately shunned him. It is at this point in our story that Charles begins working for the Wilsons, and during his employ the monster begins to travel from Ingolstadt to Geneva, learning to speak and read along the way and enduring his own adversity and hardships.

In Mary Shelley's story the monster goes from being naturally kind-hearted (albeit confused, depressed, and unable to understand or deal with his emotions) to a cold-blooded murderer. Obviously, the monster reaches a breaking point after experiencing a certain amount of rejection and pain, but some may find it a difficult leap to take a character who just tried to save a young girl's life and then have him shortly after murder Victor's youngest brother, a child. He then feels comfortable going on a killing spree, murdering innocent people without remorse, all in the name of revenge upon his maker.

The last chapter of *Rampant* serves as a possible alternative, or additional content, to explain that final jump the monster makes into becoming, essentially, a true *monster*, one willing to end others' lives. While traveling to Geneva in *Frankenstein*, it is quite possible, geographically, that the monster would pass through Cologny, where our story is taking place, and therefore the timing could very well line up with Charles wolf-man transformation. I felt if he could kill Charles out of mercy, while still in a state of emotional anguish with a growing level of anger, that it could act as a stepping-stone to murdering the child William, adding a level of plausibility.

It must be said that although the monster's appearance in *Rampant* does take place during a specific time in Mary Shelley's story, between the monster being shot in the shoulder and him killing William in Geneva, it is not technically a perfectly seamless tie-in. In *Frankenstein*, Henry arrives in Ingolstadt the morning after Victor created the monster, who has already left Victor's apartment and is wandering alone and frightened. In *Rampant* it can be assumed that if the monster left Ingolstadt the same day that Henry arrived, he would have to reach Cologny in a period of about one month, as the story only takes place a little over one full moon cycle. But in Mary Shelley's novel it takes the monster several months to reach Geneva where he kills William, so it is not likely that he could travel to Cologny, so geographically close to Geneva, in a period of one month. The difference between the stories lies here: in *Rampant*, Victor has already created the monster and it has been traveling for some time before Henry arrived in Ingolstadt. I made this small change to benefit my own story, as it was quite useful having Henry be able to be present at the funeral in Chapter 4, and would make no real impact on Mary Shelley's narrative.

It was important to me that I treat Mary Shelley's story and the characters of Henry and the monster with the utmost respect. My werewolf story would have been fine without the *Frankenstein* connection; I didn't require it, but I wanted to apply aspects of her story as a tribute to her masterpiece of a novel and as a nod to a legendary creation that horror fans might enjoy seeing in the story. To show proper consideration for her work, I tried to capture Henry's personality with precise accuracy, and I was careful to describe the monster exactly as he appeared in her novel, instead of utilizing the appearance popularized by the Universal film. For those of you who have never read the novel *Frankenstein*, I hope *Rampant* may serve as the necessary inspiration for you to do so.

- Joshua Werner

AFTERWORD: THE FACT INSIDE THE FICTION

One of the wonderful things about fiction is the complete lack of inhibition the writer can feel in creating the story, especially one with supernatural elements such as this one. The writer can invent back-stories however he or she sees fit, allowing for a great convenience when threading together a coherent narrative. But much of *Rampant* was the product of tireless research, in an effort to bring together elements of real history, existing legends, and my own brand of fiction. So I thought I'd share with you some of the facts embedded in my fiction, so that if something piques your interest you're able to research it and learn more.

Cologny

The small village of Cologny where our story takes place is indeed a real place in the Canton of Geneva in Switzerland. It is also on the bank of Lake Geneva and its inhabitants speak French, English, and German. The layout for the village I created is entirely fictitious, in respects to the forests, buildings, orchard, valley, and mountains. But the municipality of Cologny that exists today does have some forest land as well as land dedicated to agricultural use.

The Consumption

The illness that Charles' father suffers from in the story is Tubercle Bacillus, more commonly referred to as Tuberculosis. It's an infectious disease that often attacks the lungs and causes a chronic cough and fever. It was often called "Consumption" because of the excessive weight loss that accompanied the symptoms. Tuberculosis was exceptionally prevalent in the 18th century.

The Werewolf Trials

In the story I mention the "werewolf trials" that took place in Charles' area. Yes, these were *real!* The area that is now Switzerland was the first to torture and burn werewolves, in 1407, and they held many werewolf trials in the 15th, 16th, and 17th centuries, finally ending them in the 18th century. The werewolf trials commonly overlapped with the witch trials, as it was believed most werewolves were given their power by the devil, which in turn counted as witchcraft.

The manner in which they were tortured and executed is also described accurately in *Rampant*. If you'd like to research werewolf trials I recommend looking up the 1589 trial of Peter Stumpp, you can do a search in your favorite search engine for "the Werewolf of Bedburg." It's one of the best-documented werewolf trials and also one of the absolute craziest. I highly recommend reading up on it. Another trial worth researching is the 1651 trial of "Hans the Werewolf."

The Wilson Clan and Prince Wolf

There are two principal family lines bearing the name Wilson in Scotland. The much older of the two represent a branch of the House of Inness in Banffshire. These early Nordic Wilsons do indeed descend from a Danish tribe who followed a 9th century Danish Prince of the Royal House of Norway named Wolf. You can learn more about King Harold of Norway, Prince Wolf, and the Viking expansion by researching the Viking Sagas and the Orkneyinga Sagas. The Wilson surname from this line started off as "Wolf's son."

It's also true that Prince Wolf gave all Wilsons possessing a grant of arms the privilege of using the golden rampant wolf on their crest. Ayrshire, as mentioned in the story, is among the places the Prince Wolf descendants settled. When William the Conqueror launched the Norman Conquest of England and battled the English earl Harold Godwinson in 1066, the Wilson clan took part in the war on the side of the Vikings. There's a lot of fascinating history regarding this clan, and I highly recommend reading up on it.

Wolfsbane

In *Rampant*, the Wilson clan ingests small doses of Wolfsbane right before their change to weaken them and keep them from running wild. They use this as a long-term survival technique, because it helps keep them hidden. If they can control their inner wolves better, then they're less likely to draw attention to themselves. The direct access to Wolfsbane was the reason they chose their location in Cologny. While this is all highly fictitious, Wolfsbane itself is an interesting plant.

Aconitum, or Aconite, is a genus for many species of flowering plants, most of which are extremely poisonous. Historically, the poisons extracted from Aconite have had several uses. But one such use was indeed to kill wolves, which is how it earned the nickname "Wolfsbane."

While Wolfsbane may not have grown in Cologny, Switzerland necessarily, it does grow in windy mountainous areas in Europe. Especially damp, shady fields, such as the mountain meadow described in the story as being North of the Wilsons' mansion.

Wolves in Scotland

In the story, Lillian describes to Charles how the last of the wolves were killed in Scotland. While in actuality she was telling the fictitious tale of how the werewolves (the Wilsons) were driven out, there is actually quite a bit of truth in what she said in regard to real wolves in Scotland.

Wolves were incredibly common in Scotland, and they weren't particularly small ones either. They did dig up a lot of graves and kill a lot of people. They became such a threat to travellers in Scotland that James I passed a law that required wolf hunts in 1427. Over a century later James VI was also pushing a minimum number of wolf hunts.

Eventually every last wolf was killed in Scotland. Official Scottish records say the last wolf was killed in 1680, but there were still sightings for over a hundred years later. I recommend looking up "MacQueen of Findhorn," if you're interested in hearing some Scottish folklore on the subject. It's a fascinating tale about an old man who was said to have killed the last wolf in Scotland in 1743.

Over the past fifteen years or so there have been several people pushing to reintroduce wolves into Scotland, in hopes that wolves would help lower the extreme number of deer there. The deer population is so large that it's actually become harmful to some plants, trees, and birds. As of yet though, there are no plans (that I know of) to reintroduce wolves into Scotland, partly due to some farmers in rural areas that are concerned about the wolves killing their livestock.

Magical Wolf Skins

Michael tells Charles a story about Sigmund and Sinfjotli finding magical wolf skins that curse the wearers to become wolves. This is an actual Norse myth, with Sigmund being a popular character in the Volsung saga, appearing as both a hero and an outlaw. In some versions of the story they find the skins in an abandoned hunting cabin, and in other versions of the story they murder the owners in their sleep and steal them. Much of the Viking Age saw a belief in wolf-men due to numerous Norse myths.

The Wulver

Michael also tells Charles the tale of the Wulver, which came from folklore from the Shetland Islands off the coast of Scotland. The tale told in *Rampant* is accurate to the real folklore, except the real story described it as looking like a man's body, not a woman's. Irish folklore has tales of a similar wolf creature called the Faoladh.

I hope reading about some of the real history and cultural mythology that was built into the story of *Rampant* was interesting for you. And hopefully may even cause you to look up further information on some of the subjects to learn more! Thank you ever so much for reading this book, and if you enjoyed it, it would mean the world to me if you'd recommend it to a friend!

Much love,
- Joshua Werner

RAMPANT

ABOUT THE AUTHOR

Joshua Werner is an illustrator, author, designer, and all-around creative mastermind looking to infect the world with his special brand of eccentricity. He resides with his family in America's Mitten, where many have dubbed him the nickname "Frantic," making his living by sitting awkwardly in a chair for long hours, working his right hand until it breaks open and bleeds awesomeness out onto paper. If you'd like to read more of Josh's fiction, try his books *Adoration for the Dead* and *The Brutality of Fact*, and you can find some of his short stories in the anthologies *Alter Egos* and *Feast of the Dead*, all of which are available from Source Point Press.
You can check out some of his artwork at:
www.AsFallLeaves.com
www.facebook.com/AsFallLeaves
www.twitter.com/JoshuaFrantic

And, of course, be sure to try out some of the refreshingly awesome books coming out from Source Point Press:
www.SourcePointPress.com
www.facebook.com/SourcePointPress
www.twitter.com/SourcePtPress

Great Lakes
Great Connections
Great Talent
GREAT COMICS

MICHIGAN COMICS COLLECTIVE
MICHIGANCOMICSCOLLECTIVE.ORG

@MiComicCollect
FACEBOOK/MichiganComicsCollective
INFO@MichiganComicsCollective.Org

GET CONNECTED

Do you like being scared? Do you like scaring others?

Then the Great Lakes Association of Horror Writers Wants You!

Are you a writer, an artist, or just a fan of horror, science fiction, mystery, dark humor, and thrillers? Do you just like the strange, the dark, and the weird?

Then we may be who you're looking for.

If monsters, murder, and mayhem are your favorite literary playgrounds, then we are that haunted home away from home for you.

EMAIL US AT:
updates@greatlakeshorror.com

www.greatlakeshorror.com

SOURCE POINT PRESS
YOUR SOURCE FOR HORROR!
WWW.SOURCEPOINTPRESS.COM

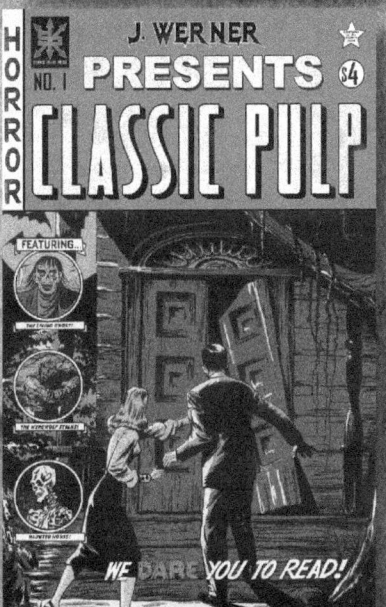

FEAST OF THE DEAD
TALES BEYOND YOUR WORST NIGHTMARES!
SHOCK! TERROR! SUSPENSE!

FEAST OF THE DEAD: HORS D'OEUVRES
TERROR IN BITE-SIZE PORTIONS
PACKED WITH STORIES, POETRY, ARTWORK, INTERVIEWS

ADORATION FOR THE DEAD
J. WERNER
TALES OF INSANITY AND TERROR

J. WERNER PRESENTS CLASSIC PULP
NO. 1 — HORROR — $4
FEATURING...
WE DARE YOU TO READ!

OTHER TITLES AVAILABLE FROM SOURCE POINT PRESS

BOOKS
Alter Egos: Volume One
Alter Egos: Volume Two
Feast of the Dead
Feast of the Dead: Hors D'oeuvres
Adoration for the Dead: Tales of Insanity and Terror
Kaiju
Weird Little Kid
Delightfully Wicked Poetic Tales
A Curious Volume of Forgotten Lore

COMIC BOOK SERIES
Jack of Spades
Serial
Classic Pulp
Source Point Presents

www.SourcePointPress.com
SourcePointPress.Storenvy.com
www.facebook.com/SourcePointPress
www.twitter.com/SourcePtPress

RAMPANT